Andrea Zimmerman
& David Clemesha

Digger Man

Henry Holt and Company

New York

SQUARE
FISH

Imprints of Macmillan
175 Fifth Avenue
New York, New York 10010
mackids.com

Henry Holt® is a registered trademark of Henry Holt and Company, LLC. *Publishers since 1866.*
Square Fish and the Square Fish logo are trademarks of Macmillan and are used by Henry Holt
and Company under license from Macmillan.

Library of Congress Cataloging-in-Publication Data
Zimmerman, Andrea Griffing.
Digger man / Andrea Zimmerman and David Clemesha.
p.   cm.
Summary: A young boy imagines how he will use his digger to make a park
where he and his little brother can play.
[1. Steam shovels—Fiction. 2. Brothers—Fiction. 3. Imagination—Fiction.]
I. Clemesha, David. II. Title.
PZ7.Z618 Di 2003   [E]—dc21   2002010856

Originally published in the United States by Henry Holt and Company
The artists used acrylic on Bristol paper to create the illustrations for this book.
First Square Fish Edition: December 2011
Square Fish logo designed by Filomena Tuosto

ISBN 978-0-8050-6628-9 (Henry Holt hardcover)
15   14   13   12   11   10   9

ISBN 978-0-8050-8203-6 (Square Fish paperback)
15   14   13   12   11   10   9   8   7

AR: 1.7

To Barbara Cooper,
who answers her calling
beautifully, and to all the other
preschool teachers like her

I love diggers.

My brother is too little, so he doesn't know . . .

My digger will be powerful. I'll wear a hard hat and heavy digger-man boots.

I will work while my brother sleeps.

I will scoop up rocks.

I will push mud.

Sometimes my mom and dad can bring
my brother to see me.

Maybe I can give my brother
a ride in the digger.

I'll honk the horn and
flash the lights for him.

One day I will dig a big hole
to make a pond.

CAUTION CAUTION CAUTION CAUTION CAUTION CAUTION

I will push the extra dirt to make a big hill.

I will plant trees and make a playground.
It will be a park. My digger park.

My brother and I can play there.

I will always have a lot of work
to do with my digger.

CAUTION   CAUTION   CAUTION   CAUTION   CAUTION   C

As soon as my brother gets bigger,
I will teach him . . .

. . . so he can be a digger man, too.